Cookie Becker
Casts a Spell

Cookie Becker Casts a Spell

by Lee Glazer

Illustrated by Margot Apple

Little, Brown and Company

BOSTON   TORONTO

FIRST EDITION

Library of Congress Cataloging in Publication Data

Glazer, Lee.
    Cookie Becker casts a spell.

    SUMMARY: When unattractive Cookie Becker loses the
lead in the class play to another girl, she puts a
curse on the production.
    [1. School stories] I. Apple, Margot. II. Title.
PZ7.G48144Co   [E]   79-13268
ISBN 0-316-31582-6

HOR

Published simultaneously in Canada
by Little, Brown & Company (Canada) Limited

PRINTED IN THE UNITED STATES OF AMERICA

For my parents

AT FIRST, nobody in Mrs. Mack's class was looking forward to the First Annual Spring Festival.

Nobody, that is, except Cookie Becker.

Mrs. Mack clasped her hands together tightly as if she could hardly keep from clapping. "This is going to be the best Spring Festival the Bunker Hill Middle School has ever had!" she said.

"This is the *only* Spring Festival the Bunker Hill Middle School has ever had," Ronald Ellis pointed out.

"Every class will have its own salute to spring," Mrs. Mack explained. "Some will sing a song about spring, some will do a dance of welcome to spring, some will present a short skit . . ."

"Sounds dumb," whispered Tod Rubin.

"Pass these back, please," said Mrs. Mack. "This is the script for the little play we're going to do. You can look it over quickly and decide what part you'd like to try for."

Cookie Becker was the tallest — and fattest — girl in the class, and she sat in the last seat of the last row. So by the time the script got to her, most of the other kids were already reading it.

"This is baby stuff," grumbled Ronald.

"It's all about birds and flowers and little raindrops," complained Danny Chang. "I'm not going to be no daffydill."

"You could be a stinkweed," said Tod.

Cookie Becker blocked her ears with her hands so she wouldn't hear the chatter around her. She leaned over her desk to read the play.

She noticed right away that two characters had the biggest parts. One was the boy who fell asleep in the middle of winter and had "The Dream of Spring," which was the name of the play. The other was the Head Raindrop.

Mrs. Mack called the Head Raindrop "Raindrop Number One," but Cookie knew it was the Head Raindrop because it had the most lines, and bossed all the other raindrops around.

Instead of reading the whole play, Cookie just read all the words that the Head Raindrop had to say.

"Do we have to know this by heart?" asked Lisa Wynne.

"It's a very short play," said Mrs. Mack. "No one will have that much to learn."

Except the Head Raindrop, thought Cookie. That's *my* part.

Suddenly Cookie was as excited about the Spring Festival as Mrs. Mack was. Maybe no one else in the class wanted to be in the play, but Cookie was used to being on the outside of things. Except for Doreen Smith, who sometimes let Cookie eat lunch with her, there wasn't one person that Cookie could call her friend.

She pretended she didn't care that nobody liked her, as long as they left her alone. Most of the time they did, because Cookie Becker was so big that the kids were afraid to get her too angry. All she had to do was sit on a kid, and *splat* — he'd be squashed flatter than a pancake.

Cookie waved her hand.

Mrs. Mack looked surprised. Cookie hardly ever raised her hand except to ask if she could go to the Girls' Room.

"Mrs. Mack, I want to try out for the Head Raindrop. I mean, Raindrop Number One."

Ronald Ellis gave a nasty little laugh. "If that raindrop fell on you, you'd drown." A few kids near him snickered nervously. Cookie glared at Ronald. The laughing stopped. Ronald looked down at his desk and pretended he hadn't said anything.

"I'm glad to see someone taking an interest in our festival," Mrs. Mack said. "We'll have the tryouts for the raindrops first, since Cookie is so eager for a part."

Two other girls wanted to try out for the part of the Head Raindrop. One was Lisa Wynne and the other was Jeanette Jackson.

"You were so worried about learning things by heart," Cookie muttered angrily to Lisa.

"I wasn't *worried*," Lisa said. "I was just wondering."

Cookie read first. She stood in front of the room with the whole class watching her. She began to feel uncomfortable. She knew everyone was giggling at her behind their hands, just waiting for her to make a mistake.

So she read very slowly and carefully. But she tried to read with feeling, like an actor. It was harder than she thought. And she *had* to get this part. She just *had* to.

If she was the star of "The Dream of Spring," her parents would see her in a play for the first time. They had never been to any plays Cookie had been in. That was because she never had a big part. They were much too busy to spend a whole hour just to hear Cookie say one line, or even worse, to watch her stand and move her lips with the chorus.

Cookie's father was the superintendent of the apartment house where they lived, and her mother was almost as much the "super" as he was. She could fix light switches and unclog sinks and replace windowpanes. The two of them always seemed to be busy in someone else's apartment.

But if Cookie was the star of this play, they'd have to come. They'd be so proud of her!

"Little children," Cookie read loudly, "love to splash through us when we make piddles in the street."

The class burst into roars of laughter.

Cookie's face burned red.

"Puddles!" she shouted. "I meant *puddles!*"

The class was laughing too hard to hear her.

Cookie wanted to run out of the room. She couldn't beat up the whole class, though that was what she felt like doing.

Mrs. Mack rapped on her desk for quiet. "That was fine, Cookie. You may sit down now. Lisa, it's your turn."

The tryouts took all morning.

Cookie could hardly keep still. She told herself she would never get the part. She had read badly. Mrs. Mack would be afraid she'd mess up the play at the Festival.

Still, she couldn't help picturing herself as the Head Raindrop, the *star*. Her parents would clap for her and tell people in the audience, "That's our daughter!"

Just when Cookie felt she couldn't wait another moment, Mrs. Mack announced, "Raindrop Number One, Lisa Wynne."

Cookie nearly jumped out of her seat in rage.

"Raindrop Number Four, Cookie Becker."

"But Raindrop Number Four only has one line!" Cookie howled. "That's not fair!"

The lunch bell rang.

Cookie grabbed her lunch bag. Nearly blind with anger, she shoved people out of her way as she charged for the door.

"Cookie!" cried Mrs. Mack. "Now, Cookie, you must be a good sport . . ."

Cookie turned to face the class. Her eyes were blazing and her face was like a thundercloud.

"*A curse!*" she said wildly. "I put a curse on your stupid Spring Festival. An evil spell will fall on all of you!"

With that, she turned and ran out of the room.

Cookie Becker didn't know the first thing about curses, hexes, or evil spells. She had yelled her curse without thinking. But she was so angry at Mrs. Mack and the class that she was determined to carry out her threat.

She remembered some things she had seen
on TV, and came up with a few ideas of her
own.

With a Magic Marker she drew eyes and
hair on a potato and wrote "Lisa Wynne" on it.
Then she made up a spell and chanted it to the
potato.

She got a candle and scratched "Spring Festival" on it with a screwdriver, then lit the wick and watched it burn, melting the Spring Festival away. As it burned, she chanted:

"On the Spring Festival I put a hex,

"May you all turn into nervous wrecks."

Cookie spent all of the afternoon and most of the evening in her room working on her curse. She didn't even come out to watch television.

At school Cookie Becker began scaring almost everyone. Did she really know how to cast a spell? Nobody knew for sure that she *didn't*.

At least once a day she chanted her curse to Lisa:

"Lisa, Lisa, Lisa Wynne,

"You'll forget your part before you begin."

Lisa began to run away every time she saw

You'll forget your part before you begin .....

Cookie coming, but Cookie just ran after her and shouted it anyway. Lisa was good and scared.

She should be, thought Cookie. She took *my* part.

Whenever Mrs. Mack wasn't around, Cookie chanted in a deep, mean voice:

"On the Spring Festival I put a hex,

"May you all turn into nervous wrecks."

The kids complained to Mrs. Mack, and she
tried to reason with Cookie. "You know you
can't really cast a spell, don't you, Cookie?"

Cookie shrugged.

"Then why don't you stop spoiling things
for everyone?"

Everyone always spoils things for *me*, Cookie
thought. But to Mrs. Mack she said, "If I can't
really cast a spell, how can I spoil things?"

Mrs. Mack sighed. Cookie was still angry at
her.

Cookie had been the only one in the class who liked the play, and Mrs. Mack had given *her* part to someone else. So Cookie told Mrs. Mack she wouldn't be in the play at all. She even had a special curse for Mrs. Mack:

"Mrs. Mack, you have no heart,

"You'll be sorry I didn't get the part."

But she only said that one at home.

When Cookie Becker woke up on the morning of the Spring Festival it was snowing.

"What crazy weather," said Mrs. Becker.
"Snow on the first day of spring."

Cookie just looked into her cereal bowl and
smiled.

By the time she got to school, it had stopped
snowing. In the classroom, Cookie took out the
potato with Lisa's name on it. She stuck it
under Lisa's nose and whispered:

"Lisa, Lisa, Lisa Wynne,

"You'll forget your part before you begin."

Lisa gave a little scream and knocked the potato to the floor.

"Sit down, Cookie," Mrs. Mack said sharply. "And whatever that is, get rid of it."

Cookie stuck the potato back in her pocket and took her seat. Everyone looked at her nervously. Did it snow because of Cookie's curse?

Cookie just smiled.

Since the snow had stopped and the sun was shining, the principal decided to have the Festival in the schoolyard, as planned. Only it was so cold that everyone had to wear their coats and boots.

"But no one will see my costume!" wailed Lisa. "No one will know I'm a raindrop! My mother worked for days on this costume."

"I'm sure your mother wouldn't want you to get sick," said Mrs. Mack.

Lisa turned and gave Cookie a long, hard stare.

Cookie just smiled.

"We can't do our dance in boots," said Doreen. "We'll look like clodhoppers."

"I know," Mrs. Mack sighed. "It can't be helped."

The schoolyard was filled with kids. All the classes stood in a big circle around the flagpole. There were hardly any parents there at all.

Mr. Kelly's class went first. They just lined up in a row and sang "Welcome, Sweet Springtime."

Then Ms. Witmer's class recited a poem called "Ode to Spring." Nobody could understand a word they were saying.

Finally it was Mrs. Mack's class's turn.

Tod, who played the boy who fell asleep
and had the dream of spring, had to fall asleep
standing up, because Mrs. Mack wouldn't let
him lie down in the slush around the flagpole.

The kids around Cookie snickered as Tod
stood there with his eyes closed, snoring
loudly.

When it was time for Lisa's first line, Cookie held up the potato. Lisa saw it and her eyes opened wide. She hesitated, but just for a moment. Then she started saying her lines. She flashed Cookie a mean little smile. Cookie smiled back.

"Little children," said Lisa loudly, "love to splash through us when we make piddles in the street."

The audience screamed with laughter. Lisa turned bright red. She ran to hide behind the other raindrops and the laughter got louder. Mrs. Mack signaled the class to begin the dance.

Half the class sang a song called "We Love Everything about Spring." The rest of the kids did the dance. When they sang "We love the green buds on the trees, we love the feel of a soft, warm breeze," a gust of icy wind howled around the flagpole and it started snowing again.

The dancers stomped so hard in their boots that they splashed the slush on each other. Doreen slipped, and grabbed Danny Chang to keep from falling. They both crashed down hard in a puddle of melted snow.

By this time, the whole school was roaring with laughter at Mrs. Mack's class.

Mrs. Mack looked very unhappy. She bit her lip, almost as if she were trying not to cry.

At the end of the dance all the kids were supposed to throw tissue paper flowers to the audience. Only, by the time the dance was finished, the flowers were just balls of soggy Kleenex. So it looked like the kids were tossing dirty, old tissues around the schoolyard.

When the festival was over and they were back in the classroom, everyone started yelling at once about how Cookie had ruined the play.

"That's silly," said Mrs. Mack. "Cookie couldn't make it snow. It was just bad luck."

She means *good luck*, thought Cookie.

"She made me mess up my lines," said Lisa. "She put a curse on me."

"No one can put a curse on anyone," said Mrs. Mack firmly.

Cookie Becker just smiled. She didn't think she really had magic powers. But the kids thought she did and that had made them nervous. And being nervous had made them ruin the play.

Later, when Cookie was eating her lunch, alone, the pleasure of spoiling the class play faded away. What had she done except give everyone who didn't like her a new reason to hate her? Now even Doreen wouldn't let her eat lunch at her table any more. She had started this whole thing because she wanted to be the star of the play, so her parents would be proud of her. Why should they be proud of her for spoiling the Spring Festival? To make someone proud, you had to *be* something, not spoil something.

Cookie looked up and found Mrs. Mack standing next to her. Mrs. Mack must be awfully angry at her, even if she *didn't* believe in spells.

But Mrs. Mack just said, "You really wanted to be Raindrop Number One, didn't you, Cookie?"

Suddenly there were tears trickling down Cookie's cheeks.

"*Yes,*" she said, swiping them away. "That was all I *ever* wanted. I'm sorry I made you feel bad."

"I'm sorry I made *you* feel bad," Mrs. Mack said gently. "I didn't really understand. But I do now. We're going to do another play for Flag Day, though. There's a part in it that's just right for you."

Cookie looked up at Mrs. Mack. She could hardly believe it. She was going to get a second chance! She might be the *star* after all!

"Oh, thank you, Mrs. Mack!"

Mrs. Mack grinned. "No more spells, now."

Cookie shook her head hard. "No more spells," she promised. "Except during spelling lessons!"